5/16

D1540466

WHEN I'M A MONSTER LIKE YOU, DAD!

WHEN I'M A MONSTER LIKE YOU, DAD!

David O'Connell

illustrated by
Francesca Gambatesa

HarperCollins *Children's Books*

Daddy, your teeth are jagged and sharp!
Are they for chomping and munching?

For chewing up houses and grinding up cars?
I love to hear the crunching!

I can't wait to be big and bad,
When I'm a monster like you, Dad!

Son, teeth are for smiling when saying, *"Hello!"*
For showing you're happy or pleased.

When hearing a joke you give a wide grin,
You young ones just love to be teased!

*I couldn't wait to **play** and have **fun**,*
When I was small like you, Son.

Daddy, your tail is scaly and long!
Is it for **whipping** and **thrashing**?

For sneaking round corners
and snatching up snacks?

As well as being quite...

...dashing!

I can't wait to be big and bad,
When I'm a monster like you, Dad!

No, Son, tails are for chasing—our favorite sport!
A jump-rope all ready-made!
For swinging from one tree to next in the woods,
So many great games to be played!

I couldn't wait to **play** and have *fun*,
When I was small like you, Son.

Daddy, your eyes are yellow and fierce!

Are they
for glaring
and spying?

For searching for secrets
lost under the bed.

Can you spot me?
I love to go prying!

I can't wait to be big and bad,
  When I'm a monster like you, Dad!

No, Son, eyes are for hunting for friends high and low.

It's the thrill of the game hide-and-seek!

For looking for presents
tucked out of sight,
When you know that you just
shouldn't peek.

I couldn't wait to **play** and have **fun,**
When I was small like you, Son.

Daddy, your arms are enormous and strong!
Are they for thumping and smashing?

For ripping up bridges
and pulling up trees?
And sending them flying
and
crashing?

I can't wait to be big and bad,
When I'm a monster like you, Dad!

My Son, arms are for climbing up hillsides,
Hang on little one; it's quite steep!

For throwing a ball just as far as you can...

And to hug Teddy when you're asleep.

I couldn't wait to **play** and have *fun,*
When I was small like you, Son.

I can wait to be **big**.

I can wait to be **bad**.

It's nice to be small, I'll admit.

But...

...grown-up monsters must have so much fun!

Well *maybe* we do...

For Freddie—D.O'C.

To my monster family and
to the hairiest of all: Dad!—F.G.

First published in Great Britain in paperback by HarperCollins Children's Books in 2016

This edition first published in hardback by HarperCollins Children's Books in 2016

1 3 5 7 9 10 8 6 4 2

ISBN: 978-0-00-816724-0

HarperCollins Children's Books is a division of HarperCollins Publishers Ltd.

Text copyright © David O'Connell 2016
Illustrations copyright © Francesca Gambatesa 2016

Visit our website at www.harpercollins.co.uk

Printed and bound in China